COLE FAMILY

Papa

Dock

Maude

Hilda

Al

Nelle

Ruble

Hob

Fos

Tony

Hazel

HILDA
A VERY LOYAL GOAT

Donated to all the
children (young + old) at
the Thould library.
May you keep your belief
in yourself, no matter what
is said about you.

the illustrator—

Jennifer Julich

OCTOBER 2009

Published by Next Chapter Press

PO Box 1937

Boca Grande, FL 33921

Publisher's Cataloging-Publication Data

Bryan, Jennifer Liu.

Hilda, a very loyal goat / Jennifer Liu Bryan. – Boca Grande, FL : Next Chapter Press, 2009.

p. ; cm.

Summary: A loyal goat finds trouble and then joy as he follows his best friend to school one day.

ISBN: 978-0-9816265-1-2

1. Goats—Juvenile fiction. I. Title.

PZ7.B79 2009

[E]—dc22   2009927878

Creative Director: Bob Robbins

Cover and Interior Design: Electra Communications, www.ElectraCommunications.ca

Illustrator: Jenniffer Julich, www.jnnffr.com

Printed in Singapore

13 12 11 10 09 • 5 4 3 2 1

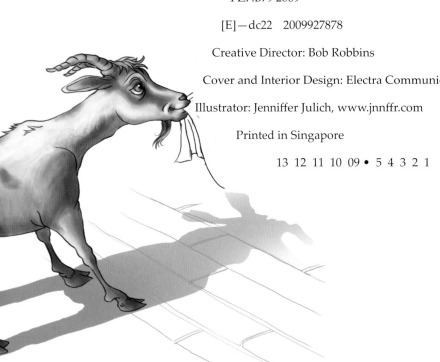

HILDA
A VERY LOYAL GOAT

Jennifer Liu Bryan
Illustrations by Jenniffer Julich

Next Chapter Press
Boca Grande, Florida, USA

*To my family
for their love and support*

Hilda was a very loyal goat... though sometimes he was called meddlesome.

When he was very small, he came to live with the Cole family. His owner was a little girl named Ruble, and he loved her very much. Ruble had always wanted a best friend named Hilda. So, even though her new pet was a *boy* goat, she decided to call him Hilda just the same.

Hilda didn't mind. Ruble liked his name, so Hilda liked it too. He was a very loyal goat.

Hilda tried to be a good goat, but sometimes it was hard. After all, Hilda was a curious goat.

He liked to butt things with his head. He liked to taste things with his tongue. He liked to sneak out of his pen. And he liked to go wherever Ruble was going.

He was a very loyal goat.

One morning, Hilda woke very early, even before the sun peeked over the big mountains that surrounded the Cole house. He tried, but he just couldn't rest. He was too excited about the day to come.

3

The Cole house was dark. Ruble was still asleep. For a while, Hilda kicked a pail around his pen. Ruble did not wake up.

Then he gnawed on the latch to the pen until he could push the gate open. Ruble did not wake up.

Then he walked up and down the steps on the Cole family's porch. Still, Ruble did not wake up.

At last, Hilda thought he'd have to wake up Ruble himself.

He gently pushed open the door and trotted through the family room into the bedroom where six of the nine Cole children slept. Ruble was fast asleep.

Hilda shyly tugged at Ruble's quilt. Ruble did not stir. Hilda softly snorted. Ruble did not move. Hilda gently pushed Ruble with his nose. Ruble just rolled over.

Boy, Hilda thought, Ruble sure is hard to wake up.

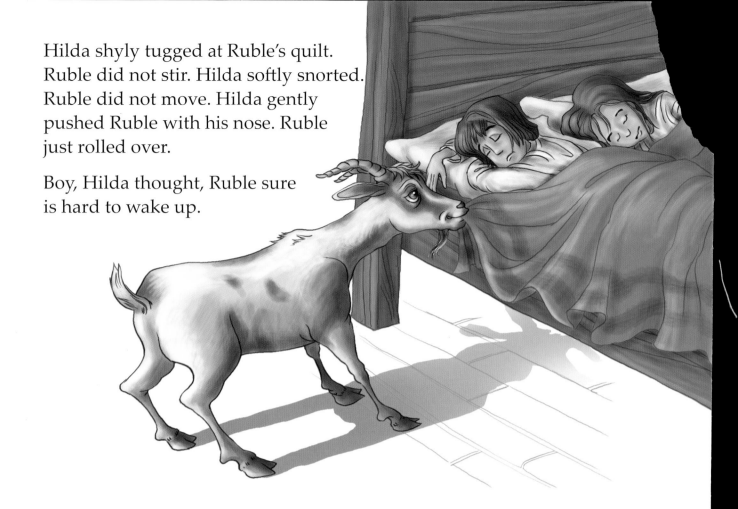

He bleated more loudly. Ruble's brothers and sisters stirred, and her brother Al even looked down from his bunk bed at Hilda. "Meddlesome goat," he muttered sleepily.

But Ruble still did not wake up.

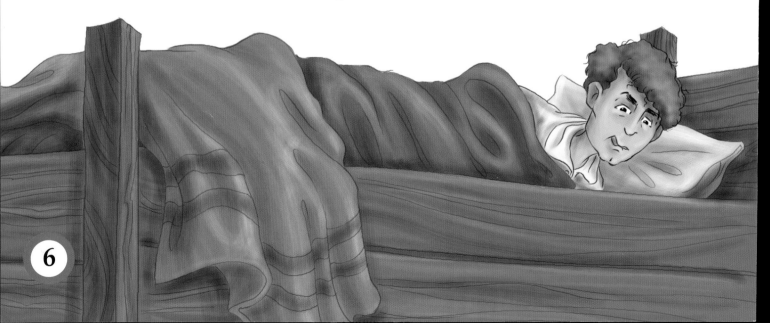

Hilda sighed. He supposed he'd have to wait until Ruble woke up on her own. He started to back out of the room, still watching to see whether Ruble might wake up. He backed up a little, then a little more, then a little more, and...

CRASH!

Hilda bumped into one of the children's chests of clothes and knocked it over, spilling a pitcher of water.

Hilda leapt forward in surprise, but his hooves tangled in a quilt. He stumbled and crashed into Ruble's bed, bleating in panic.

She fell out of bed with a *thud*. "Ooof," cried Ruble.

Ruble's brothers and sisters were now awake too, and they started yelling in confusion. Hilda was awfully excited. He scampered about, his hooves still tangled in the quilt, the spilled clothes scattering about the floor and into the puddle of water.

"Ruble! Get your goat out of here!" yelled one of her brothers.

"What a mess!" another exclaimed.

"My clothes!" cried Ruble's sister Nelle, looking at the wet tangle on the floor.

Finally, Hilda felt a familiar firm hand on his head. It was Ruble. He stopped his kicking and bleating. He looked up at her, glad that she was awake at last.

But Ruble did not look glad. Ruble looked cross.

"Hilda," she said sternly, "you are a meddlesome goat! What a mess you've made. Back to your pen now."

Hilda ducked his head in shame. He hadn't meant to make such a mess. He'd only wanted to play with Ruble. He was a very loyal goat.

9

Ruble led Hilda back to his pen and shut the gate firmly. Hilda
could only watch when Ruble and her brothers and sisters left
a little while later to go to school. Ruble did not stop to pet
Hilda's head as usual.

She must be very cross indeed, thought Hilda.

He chewed the gate's latch while he thought. What could he do to make it up to Ruble?

At that moment, the latch popped open. That was it, Hilda thought. He would follow Ruble to school and keep her company. He trotted happily out of the gate.

GRRRRR! A loud rumble startled him.

GRRRRR! There it was again. Hilda looked down at his belly. GRRRRR! said his tummy once more. In all the excitement, Hilda had forgotten to eat his breakfast, and Ruble's school was a long walk away.

Hilda looked around.

He paused in front of the leafy green tops of carrots that Mama had planted. GRRRRR! said his tummy. No, no, Hilda shook his head. He was definitely not allowed to eat from Mama's garden. But perhaps… Hilda spied among the sweet vegetables a familiar and ugly spindly leaf.

Hilda knew this plant grew all over the mountain, though not usually in Mama's garden. It was bitter and wild tasting. Hilda liked it very much, but he doubted that the Coles did. Perhaps if he ate only a few...

GRRRRR! said his stomach encouragingly.

Hilda climbed into the garden, his quick tongue picking out the spindly plant from among the vegetables. He was careful not to trample anything, and to eat only this plant.

The warm sun felt soothing, and he walked among the rows, chewing the spindly leaves happily. That is, until he heard Mama's shout.

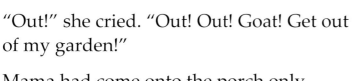

"Out!" she cried. "Out! Out! Goat! Get out of my garden!"

Mama had come onto the porch only to spy Hilda grazing in her garden. She shook her broom impatiently at him. "Out!"

Hilda bleated in surprise and made a great leap out of the garden. He opened his mouth to show that he'd eaten only the bitter plant, but Mama did not understand. She shook her broom again. "Meddlesome Hilda! Stay out of my garden!"

Seeing the broom swaying in her hand, Hilda scampered quickly down the road toward school.

Mama was still shaking her head when Hilda turned to look back. Boy, Hilda thought, I can't do anything right today. He heaved a great goat sigh. It made him sad to be scolded so. After all, he was a very loyal goat.

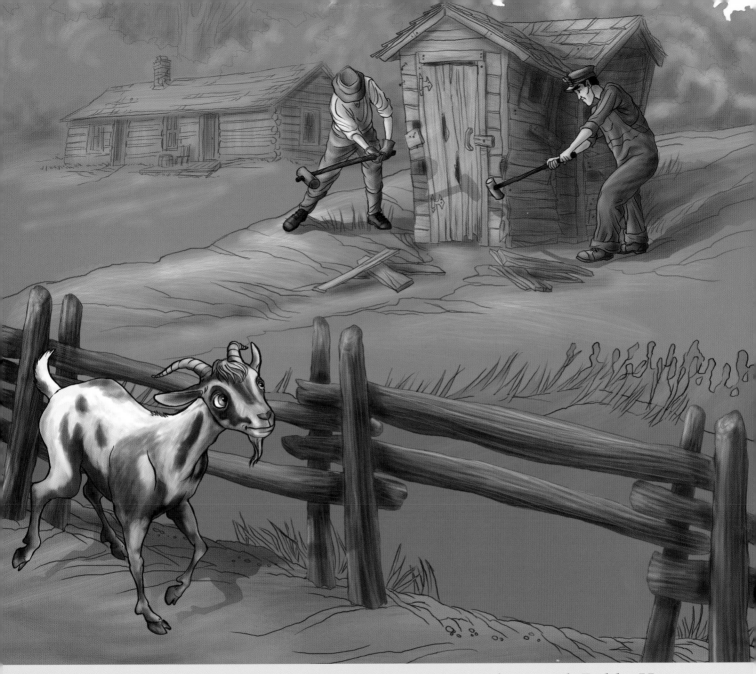

Hilda hurried down the mountain, hoping to catch up with Ruble. He stopped short when he heard Papa Cole's familiar voice.

It was coming from a neighbor's yard. Hilda watched in fascination as Papa Cole and Ruble's oldest brother, Dock, swung heavy mallets at an old shed.

Papa and Dock must be helping out Mr. Lawson, a neighbor who had been injured in the coal mine, thought Hilda. He watched as the two Coles – Papa dressed in his mining gear – tried to knock down the shed.

"I think we'll have to leave it, Papa," Dock said. "This shed just doesn't want to come down quick. We'll try again after you get home from work. Let's tell Mr. Lawson we'll be back."

The two went into the house, and Hilda approached the shed with interest. After all, Hilda was a curious goat. It was just like his shed at the Cole house.

Hilda suddenly bleated and kicked his feet in excitement. He knew how to help! He had a lot of practice butting things with his head. He was sure that he could knock down the old shed with a few well-placed blows.

Hilda backed up and lowered his head, keeping his eyes on the shed. Then he surged forward and, with a great bleat, hurled himself toward the shed.

THUMP!

The structure rattled and swayed, but did not fall. Hilda looked on with delight. He backed up once again, and then sprang forward at full speed.

THUMP!

The shed swayed again and leaned heavily to one side. It was almost ready to fall!

Hilda backed up one more time. He set his shoulders determinedly. He kicked the dirt a few times. And then he raced forward with all his might.

KER-THWUMP!

The loud sound caused Papa to rush out of the house. He was surprised to see Hilda standing in the yard, seeming to attack Mr. Lawson's shed.

"Hilda!" Papa cried. "What are you doing here? Get on up to the house! Shoo now! Go on, git!"

"What's going on?" asked Dock, joining his father. "Oh," he said, seeing Hilda, "it's that meddlesome goat of Ruble's."

Hilda looked helplessly at the shed, which swayed but did not fall. He wanted to explain that he was helping to knock it down, but Papa was already ushering him out to the road. "Back to the house, now! Always escaping from your pen," Papa muttered, wagging his finger. "You are a meddlesome goat."

Hilda walked away, heaving another great goat sigh. It seemed he could not do anything right today! First Ruble was cross with him, then Mama shook a broom at him, and now Papa and Dock shooed him away! He stood for a moment, his head down, feeling bad.

Just then Hilda heard hurried footsteps headed down the mountain. He turned to look and saw Ruble's younger brother Hob dashing down the path.

"Hilda! What are you doing here?" Hob ran up to the goat.

"I'm late for school! Do you want to walk with me?" Hilda snorted in agreement and began to trot faster. "What's worse, I didn't finish all my schoolwork. I'm really going to be in trouble," Hob moaned.

Hilda bleated in happiness at seeing Hob. Now here was a good deed he could do: He would cheer Hob up. And he was very glad to have a companion. After all, he was a very loyal goat.

He thought he might play a game he played with Ruble sometimes. First he nipped at Hob's shirt, untucking it. Hob laughed.

Then Hilda nibbled at his shoes. Hob dodged playfully out of the way.

Next Hilda tugged at Hob's overalls.

Hob giggled.

Hilda was getting very excited at this fun game. Every time he nipped at Hob's clothing, Hob would shriek with laughter.

They were a raucous pair as they skipped down the road, emitting howls of laughter and loud bleats.

Hilda spied Hob's school bag, slung over his shoulder. Sheets of paper tantalizingly poked out.

Hilda thought he would grab one and nibble that, too.

Hilda tugged out a sheet and chewed it thoughtfully, savoring the taste of a new object. He bumped his head into Hob, expecting more peals of laughter, but Hob's face darkened.

"No, Hilda, no!" he cried, as he removed the remaining bits of paper from Hilda's mouth.

"Oh, no! That was my schoolwork! The teacher is really going to give it to me now! Oh, you are a meddlesome goat. Why did you have to eat that, Hilda?" Hob buried his face in his hands.

Hilda ducked his head in shame. Oh no! He'd messed up yet again. Nothing could go right this day!

The two of them were at the doors to the schoolhouse, and Hob ran in, clutching the crumpled paper, not looking back at the forlorn goat.

Hilda kicked the ground in frustration. This day was just one disaster after another!

First Ruble was cross with him for waking her up and trampling Nelle's clothes. Then Mama was upset with him for eating from her vegetable garden. Then Papa and Dock chased him from the neighbor's yard when he was only trying to help. Now he'd ruined Hob's schoolwork.

Hilda peeked through the schoolhouse window and saw Ruble's dark head turned toward the blackboard. He heaved another goat sigh.

He didn't want to spoil Ruble's day, too. He wouldn't interrupt class or make Ruble angry with him. He'd wait until the school bell rang for lunch.

He settled down to take a nap near a shade tree by the school, but he was as sad as a loyal goat could be.

Hilda tried so hard to be good and loyal, but now it seemed that everyone in the Cole family was cross with him. Everyone had called him meddlesome, even his best friend Ruble. Hilda always thought of himself as a very loyal goat, but maybe he really was just meddlesome. Hilda sniffed and pawed at the ground. At last he found a place to rest and settled down to a fitful, unhappy sleep.

Ruble's small, soft hands around his head awakened him with a start.

The afternoon sun was high and bright above the peak of the mountain. Hilda had slept through the whole morning. "Oh, Hilda!" Ruble exclaimed. "Am I ever glad to see you! What a day I've had at school. I couldn't spell and I didn't understand the sums. And I lost the ribbon that Maude gave me to wear in my hair." She threw her arms around Hilda's neck. "I'm awfully glad that my best friend was here to meet me!"

Hilda bleated his happiness. "And I'm sorry I was cross with you this morning," Ruble continued. "I know you only wanted to wake me. You are a very loyal goat."

Ruble happily took Hilda's lead and, with her brothers and sisters, began to skip up the mountain toward home.

Hurried footsteps caused Hilda to turn. Hob was running toward him. Last time Hilda had seen him, he'd looked positively gloomy. Now, though, a big smile lit up his face.

27

"Hilda! Ruble! Wait! Wait!" he cried. He patted Hilda's head vigorously and Hilda bleated his astonishment.

"You're a genius goat, Hilda," he said. "I didn't get in trouble at all for my schoolwork!

"I hadn't finished it, you know. So when the teacher collected it, I had to tell her that a goat ate it. She didn't believe me, but then I showed her that you were sleeping by the school. She even laughed! Can you believe it?"

Hob's laughter bubbled up like a spring. "What a funny thing!

"I'm sorry I was mad at you, Hilda. You can eat my schoolwork anytime, loyal old pal!"

Ruble shook her head in amusement and whispered to Hilda, "Don't eat his schoolwork, Hilda. He doesn't mean it!"

When they got to Mr. Lawson's house, a voice called them over.

"Why, here comes that goat now!"

Hilda stopped in his tracks, and Ruble looked curiously at him. Ruble's brother Dock was motioning them over to the fence.

"That's some goat you've got there, Ruble. Would you believe he helped me knock down Mr. Lawson's old shed this morning?" Dock asked. "At first, Papa and I didn't know what he was up to, running into the walls like that. Turns out, it was just what was needed to bring that old thing down.

"Yup, that goat helped Mr. Lawson – and me and Papa – out a great deal," he said, smiling at Hilda. "I guess he's a pretty loyal goat after all."

Hilda bleated with pride and Ruble looked lovingly at him. Hob chimed in, "Boy, Hilda, you're a regular hero today, aren't you?"

Hilda kicked up his hooves with excitement at the praise.

But as they neared the Cole house, he began to get nervous. Mama Cole would no doubt tell Ruble that she'd chased Hilda from her garden.

He thought worriedly about the broom.

He slowed his pace even more when he saw Mama on her hands and knees working in her garden.

31

"Hello, children," Mama sang as the children hustled into the yard.

"You won't believe what Hilda did today," Ruble cried in excitement.

"Oh?" said Mama.

"He met me at school when I was having a terrible day. And he helped knock down Mr. Lawson's old shed, and Dock and Papa were real pleased," said Ruble with a grin. "And he got Hob out of trouble at school."

"Really?" said Mama, with an eyebrow raised. "Well, that's not all he did, I'm afraid."

Hilda began to back up, his eyes darting around for Mama's broom.

"He also helped me out a great deal in my garden this morning," she said to Ruble – and to Hilda's – astonishment. "Remember all those pesky dandelion weeds? Hilda ate every last one out of the garden. I'd have spent half the day weeding if it weren't for him."

Mama gave Hilda an affectionate pat on the head. "I'm only sorry I chased him off with my broom," she laughed.

"He is a good, loyal goat."

Hilda's eyes lit up at this praise. Hearing this, Ruble looked at her goat with surprise. "What an amazing day you've had, Hilda. It seems you've helped everyone out!"

Hob started to cheer, "Three cheers for Hilda, Ruble's loyal goat!" Soon Ruble's brothers and sisters picked up the call. "Hip! Hip! Hooray!"

Hilda jumped in the air in his excitement, kicking his hooves and bleating.

"I think our hero deserves a prize, don't you, Ruble?" said Mama, shaking the dirt from a thick orange carrot she'd pulled from the ground.

Hilda looked eagerly at the carrot. "I do indeed," Ruble said, holding the carrot out to Hilda. "Here's to you, Hilda," she said, handing him the carrot and giving him a tight squeeze.

Hilda gratefully took the carrot and bleated his affection for Ruble.

After all, he was a very loyal goat.

The End.

Hilda is not only a loyal goat. He is also a goat that loves to read. That's why Hilda has become a "spokesgoat" for families reading aloud together.

Hilda brings his special brand of wit and wisdom to the website, ReadAloud.org, which provides advice and information to children and families about the benefits of reading aloud together. As experts have shown, reading aloud to children not only builds their literacy skills, it also fosters a love of reading.

And Hilda should know. He is part of the Cole family – a family based on a real life clan with a long tradition of reading aloud together. When the nine Cole children were being raised in the early part of the 20th century, Mama Cole took time to read to them each night. It is the Cole family's tradition – and their stories – that inspired the creation of Hilda, ReadAloud.org, and the book, *Cole Family Christmas*.

The Cole family hopes that readers will follow not only Hilda's adventures, but also his example, and read aloud with their families today!

DATE DUE

DEC 15 2009	
OCT 2 7 2010	
APR 16 2011	
MAR 10 2012	
APR 03 2012	
JUL 24 2012	
MAR 06 2013	

GAYLORD   PRINTED IN U.S.A.